使命
MISSION

鏡頭下的堅毅與擔當
Perseverance and Commitment under the Lens

商務印書館

使命 Mission

鏡頭下的堅毅與責任
Perseverance and Commitment under the Lens

作者 Author	李秀恒 Eddy Li
翻譯 Translation	李佳燁 Natalie Li
	梁皓明 Kristie Leung
責任編輯 Managing Editor	李秀恒 Eddy Li
文字編輯 Text Writer	李佳燁 Natalie Li
美術主任 Art Director	李佳燁 Natalie Li
美術編輯 Designer	莫偉賢 Ryan Mok
	魏俊寶 Travis Ngai

出版 Publisher

商務印書館（香港）有限公司
The Commercial Press (H.K.) Ltd.
香港筲箕灣耀興道 3 號東匯廣場 8 樓
8/F., Eastern Central Plaza,
3 Yiu Hing Road, Shaukeiwan, Hong Kong
http://www.commercialpress.com.hk

印刷 Printer

永經堂印刷有限公司
Wing King Tong Printing Ltd.
香港新界荃灣德士古道 188–202 號
立泰工業中心第 1 座 3 樓
3/F., Leader Industrial Centre Phase 1,
188–202 Texaco Road, Tsuen Wan,
New Territories, Hong Kong

發行 Distributor

香港聯合書刊物流有限公司
SUP Publishing Logistics (H.K.) Limited
香港新界荃灣德士古道 220–248 號
荃灣工業中心 16 樓
16/F., Tsuen Wan Industrial Centre
220–248 Texaco Road, Tsuen Wan,
New Territories, Hong Kong

版次 Edition

2023 年 12 月第 1 版第 1 次印刷
First edition, First printing, December 2023
©2023 商務印書館 (香港) 有限公司
@2023 The Commerical Press (H.K.) Ltd.
ISBN 978 962 0767 16 6
Printed in Hong Kong

目錄 Contents

行政長官
李家超先生
大紫荊勳賢, SBS, PDSM, PMSM
The Chief Executive
The Hon John Lee Ka-chiu
GBM, SBS, PDSM, PMSM

二十大報告強調：「國家安全是民族復興的根基，社會穩定是國家強盛的前提」。維護公眾以至國家安全，絕對是任重而道遠。香港特區政府各個紀律部隊，一直肩負維持社會穩定、保障市民生命及財產安全的重責。我們的紀律部隊人員勇於承擔，堅韌不拔，竭盡所能執行職務，表現優秀，值得敬佩和表揚。

《使命——鏡頭下的堅毅與擔當》攝影集製作逾年，以鏡頭記錄保安局及其轄下的香港警務處、入境事務處、香港海關、懲教署、消防處、政府飛行服務隊、醫療輔助隊和民眾安全服務隊的日

常訓練、執勤和活動等，通過紀實攝影，把這羣無名英雄的故事和專業表現一一呈現。

我謹藉此機會，感謝所有紀律部隊人員盡忠職守，竭誠為市民服務。我亦期望市民大眾能通過攝影集，更深入了解紀律部隊的專業態度和英勇果敢的精神，珍視他們為維護公眾及國家安全而付出的努力，並與他們一起為香港和國家的繁榮安定不懈奮鬥。

序言
Foreword

The Report of the 20th National Congress emphasised that "national security is the bedrock of national rejuvenation, and social stability is a prerequisite for building a strong and prosperous China". It is a heavy responsibility to safeguard public safety and national security. The various disciplined services of the Hong Kong Special Administrative Region Government have always shouldered the duties of maintaining social stability and protecting the lives and properties of our citizens. The unwavering commitment, perseverance and dedication of disciplined services members in performing their duties definitely deserve our respect and recognition.

The production of the photobook *Mission: Perseverance and Commitment under the Lens* spanned over the course of more than a year. The photographers captured moments of daily training, operations and activities of the Security Bureau and its disciplined services, including the Hong Kong Police Force, Immigration Department, Hong Kong Customs and Excise Department, Correctional Services Department, Fire Services Department, Government Flying Service, Auxiliary Medical Service, and Civil Aid Service, presenting the stories and professional performances of these unsung heroes with documentary photographs.

I would like to express my gratitude to all disciplined services members for their dedication and diligence in serving the public. I hope that members of the public can gain a deeper understanding of the professionalism and bravery of the disciplined services through the photobook, thus valuing our disciplined services' efforts in safeguarding public safety and national security, as well as working together with them for the prosperity and stability of Hong Kong, and our country.

政務司司長
陳國基先生 GBS, IDSM, JP
The Chief Secretary for Administration
The Hon Chan Kwok-ki, GBS, IDSM, JP

香港近年歷經風雨，曾飽受「黑暴」衝擊，亦面對三年疫情挑戰；全賴國家關懷支持、社會上下群策群力，香港進入由亂到治走向由治及興的新階段，並踏上全面復常之路，而背後離不開特區政府保安局及其轄下紀律部隊和輔助部隊七萬人團隊的努力和付出。

各位同事愛國愛港，全面準確、堅定不移貫徹「一國兩制」方針。他們忠誠履職，挺身而出除暴安良，堅決有力維護國家安全和香港穩定；他們亦以民為本，專業高效為市民服務。香港有如此堅實可靠的守護者，是我們的光榮與驕傲。

當前，世界百年未見之大變局正加速演變，香港面臨的風險挑戰依然存在，要維護國家安全、守護香港安寧，特區政府各支紀律部隊及輔助部隊任重道遠。

我希望大眾通過這本相冊，能加深認識香港守護者的堅毅與擔當。我充滿信心，各支紀律部隊及輔助部隊會繼續肩負保障特區政府依法施政的中流砥柱，為國家、為香港的長治久安、繁榮發展譜寫新篇章。

Thanks to the strong support of the motherland and the concerted effort of the community at large, Hong Kong has entered a new stage of advancing from stability to prosperity – following the transition from chaos to order – and resumed full normality. The city has weathered the storm of the black-clad violence and three-year-long pandemic. The hard work and dedication of the 70 000-strong disciplined and auxiliary forces, under the leadership by the Security Bureau of the Hong Kong SAR Government, is instrumental to this transition.

With an affection for the motherland and Hong Kong, colleagues of the forces have been fully, faithfully and resolutely implementing the principle of "One Country, Two Systems". Not only do they maintain law and order to steadfastly safeguard national security and Hong Kong's stability, they also serve the public in a people-oriented, professional and efficient manner. We feel proud, and honoured, for having them as our highly reliable Hong Kong guardians.

As the world is undergoing accelerating changes unseen in a century, Hong Kong still faces risks and challenges ahead. The disciplined and auxiliary forces of the Hong Kong SAR Government shoulder the integral responsibilities, as always, of maintaining national security and Hong Kong's tranquility.

I hope that, after looking through this photo album, members of the public can get to know better the perseverance and commitment of our Hong Kong guardians. I have every confidence that, for the long-term stability and prosperity of the motherland and Hong Kong, all of our disciplined and ancillary forces will continue to underpin the law-based governance of the Hong Kong SAR Government.

保安局局長
鄧炳強先生 GBS, PDSM, JP
Secretary for Security
The Hon Tang Ping-keung, GBS, PDSM, JP

香港特區紀律部隊及輔助部隊，一直以維護國家安全和香港治安為使命。7萬人團隊憑著敢於擔當作為，砥礪堅毅前行的信心和決心，攜手築起「守護香港、保衛市民」的第一防線。無論是日常執勤，或是香港治安受到衝擊的艱難時刻，或是世紀疫情帶來的重大挑戰，抑或遭受天災突襲的緊急關頭，團隊上下始終恪盡職責、無懼無畏，赤誠為民服務，竭力為民解困，堅定擔當國家安全、香港穩定和民眾福祉的堅強守護者。

我很感激李秀恒博士及其攝影團隊，由 2022 年 9 月至 2023 年 10 月，花費整整一年時間，為紀律部隊及輔助部隊同仁留下數百幅工作剪影。鏡頭底下，有他們匯操時整齊一致的步伐，有演練時凌厲如風的行動，有安保時嚴肅戒備的神態，亦有關愛市民時和藹親切的笑容，一幀幀畫面拼湊出團隊的真實面貌，更展現出背後使命必達的堅毅與擔當。

我相信攝影冊的面世定能讓廣大市民更全面、更深入地了解紀律部隊及輔助部隊的工作。而我們團隊亦必定不負大眾所望，繼續發揮以人為本的專業精神，與市民齊心同行，攜手共建更美好的香港。

It has always been the mission of the disciplinary forces and auxiliary forces of the Hong Kong Special Administrative Region to safeguard national security and maintain public order in Hong Kong. With the courage to take up responsibilities and the confidence and determination to move forward, a team of 70,000 people work together to build the first line of defence to protect Hong Kong and its citizens. No matter during daily duties, difficult moments when Hong Kong's security is under threat, major challenges brought by the pandemic of the century, or an emergency when a natural disaster strikes, the team always fulfill their responsibilities with remarkable fortitude, serve the people wholeheartedly to relieve their difficulties, and stand firmly as a strong guardian of national security, Hong Kong's stability and people's well-being.

I am very grateful to Dr. Eddy Li Sau-hung and his photography team, who spent an entire year from September 2022 to October 2023 to capture hundreds of photos at work for colleagues in the disciplinary forces and auxiliary forces. Under the lens, we see their unison marching steps, their sharp and swift actions during drills, their serious and alert demeanor during security operations, and their kind and friendly smiles when caring for the citizens. We get a close look at the true face of the team, pieced together frame by frame to show their perseverance and commitment to achieve the mission behind.

I believe that the publication of the photo album will allow the general public to have a more comprehensive and in-depth understanding of the work of the disciplinary forces and auxiliary forces. Our team will certainly live up to public expectations, continue to display its people-oriented professionalism, and work hand in hand with the public to build a better Hong Kong.

警務處處長
蕭澤頤先生 PDSM

Commissioner of Police
Mr Siu Chak-yee, PDSM

首先，我衷心感謝香港中華文化
藝術推廣基金會推出《使命——
鏡頭下的堅毅與擔當》攝影集，
向公眾呈現保安局轄下隊伍為實
踐使命所作出的努力。

攝影集引人入勝，將讀者的視線
聚焦於各隊伍守護香港和服務市民的瞬間，令公眾有機會進一
步了解同事們在執行職務時勇於擔當及堅毅的一面，定格展現
同事們如何克服種種挑戰，完成任務。

翻閱這本攝影集，重溫警隊同事每一幅「忠誠勇毅心繫社會」
的照片，百般滋味在心頭，我看到警隊同事無懼任何困難，始
終堅守崗位，心懷使命，盡力維護國家安全，保護市民的生命
及財產安全。

入境事務處處長
郭俊峯先生 IDSM

Director of Immigration
Mr Benson Kwok Joon-fung, IDSM

作為執法與服務並重的紀律部隊，
入境事務處肩負維護國家安全的
光榮使命，守護國家南大門，秉持
「以人為本」的精神服務市民。

香港擁有「一國兩制」下「背靠祖
國、聯通世界」的獨特優勢。同時
入境處積極融入國家發展大局，不斷優化各項人才入境計劃，善
用科技提升通關效率，並着力完善陸路口岸基建設施。展望未來，
入境處定必繼續堅定不移地為國家和香港的發展保駕護航。

《使命》攝影集透過李博士的鏡頭，從多角度呈現香港紀律部隊
所承擔的使命。由此揭開香港「由治及興」的新篇章，攝影集獨
具匠心，讓一幕幕動人故事在光影之下閃耀奪目，教人永誌不忘。

First and foremost, I would like to express my profound gratitude to the Hong Kong Chinese Arts and Culture Promotion Foundation for their efforts in compiling Mission: Perseverance and Commitment under the Lens. This photo collection showcases the unwavering dedication of the disciplined services, led by the Security Bureau, in fulfilling their missions.

The collection captures the poignant moments of our disciplined service members as they protect Hong Kong and serve the public. It provides readers with a unique lens into the steadfast commitment and perseverance of these officers, highlighting their resolve to surmount an array of challenges in pursuit of successful missions.

Flipping through this collection and reflecting on every frame of photos of the Force members, who truly embody the spirit of "Serving Hong Kong with Honour, Duty and Loyalty", stirs a mix of emotions. Each captured moment serves as a testament to their tenacity and unwavering commitment, even when faced with the most formidable challenges. Fuelled by a strong sense of mission, they strive relentlessly to uphold national security and safeguard the lives and property of our citizens.

As a disciplined service which attaches equal importance to law enforcement and service delivery, the Immigration Department (ImmD) takes on the glorious mission of safeguarding national security by guarding the southern gate of the country and serving the public with a people-oriented approach.

Hong Kong has the unique advantages of enjoying strong support of the motherland and being closely connected to the world under the implementation of "one country, two systems". Meanwhile, the ImmD actively integrates itself into the overall development of the country by constantly making enhancements to various talent admission schemes, utilising technology to boost the efficiency of immigration clearance, as well as making vigorous upgrade of the infrastructures of land boundary control points. Looking ahead, the ImmD will continue to secure the development of the country and Hong Kong with unswerving devotion.

Through Dr. Li's lens, the photo book "Mission" demonstrates from a multitude of perspectives the undertaking of missions by disciplined services in Hong Kong. And now Hong Kong has just opened a new chapter from stability to prosperity, this photo book, with striking originality, vividly tells touching stories crystallised into unforgettable images, that will be forever cherished in our minds.

海關關長
何珮珊女士 CDSM

Commissioner of
Customs and Excise
Ms Louise Ho Pui-shan, CDSM

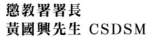

攝影是捕捉瞬間的藝術。按下快門，便攝下永恆。

李秀恒博士以一年多時間用鏡頭紀錄保安局及其轄下六支紀律部隊和兩支輔助部隊的日常訓練和執勤任務，定格最莊嚴的匯操慶典、捕捉最驚險的救急扶危、展現最動人的服務市民日常，以至《香港國安法》實施以來，見證香港「由治及興」的畫面。

李博士以相片說好海關故事，刻劃出海關人員守護國門、維護國家和香港安全的昂揚鬥志及團結精神。這本攝影集正如其書名《使命》所言，彰顯着海關全人對履行光榮使命的堅毅與擔當。

懲教署署長
黃國興先生 CSDSM

Commissioner of
Correctional Services
Mr Wong Kwok-hing, CSDSM

懲教署一直以保障公眾安全和防止罪案，締造美好香港作為使命。除致力以穩妥、安全、人道、合適和健康的環境羈管交由本署監管的人士外，本署亦積極與各界持份者攜手創造更多更生機會，並通過社區教育提倡守法和共融觀念。

跨過「由亂到治」、邁進「由治及興」的關鍵階段，懲教署樂於肩負起更大使命。除盡力教化誤入歧途的生命外，更會在社區防罪教育推陳出新，用心培育我們下一代成為愛護家國的主人翁。

謹此向《使命》的編輯團隊致意，亦希望讀者透過相冊加深認識本署任重道遠的使命。

Photography is the art of capturing moments. With the press of a shutter, eternity is captured.

Dr. Eddy Li spent over a year's time using his cameras to document the daily training and duty of the Security Bureau and the six disciplined services and two auxiliary services under its purview. He captured the solemnity of grand ceremonies, the thrilling moments of emergency rescue, and the heart-warming scenes of serving the community in their daily lives. His lenses also witnessed the transformation of Hong Kong from stability to prosperity since the implementation of the National Security Law.

Dr. Li tells good stories of the Customs and Excise Department through his photographs, depicting the unwavering determination and unity of officers in safeguarding the country's borders and ensuring the security of both the nation and Hong Kong. This photography collection, as its title "Mission" suggests, highlights the resilience and dedication of the customs personnel in fulfilling their honourable mission.

The Correctional Services Department (CSD) has always been adhering to its mission of protecting the public and preventing crime for a better Hong Kong. In addition to providing a secure, safe, humane, decent and healthy custodial environment for persons in custody, the Department is also proactive in creating more rehabilitation opportunities in collaboration with community stakeholders and promoting law-abiding and inclusive values through community education.

Following the transition from chaos to order, Hong Kong is at the crucial stage of advancing from stability to prosperity. As such, the CSD stands ready to shoulder an even greater mission. In addition to making our best endeavours to transform lives that have gone astray, we will roll out new community education initiatives on crime prevention, with a view to nurturing our next generation into masters of society with devotion to our country and home.

I would like to pay tribute to the editorial team of Mission for producing such a magnificent photo album, through which readers can gain a better understanding of our important mission.

消防處處長
楊恩健先生 FSDSM

Director of Fire Services
Mr Andy Yeung Yan-kin, FSDSM

消防處肩負「救災扶危，為民解困」的使命，一直竭力做好滅火、救援、救護和防火工作，以保護市民的生命和財產；此外，在「一國兩制」下，為配合保安和發展需要，推動香港實現由治入興的新進程，消防處除了努力維護並推廣國家安全外，亦積極宣揚愛國觀念、促進青年發展，以及建立關愛和諧社會。

攝影集中的實況照片，透過李秀恒博士的專業視角，真實而又深刻地向大眾呈現出消防處忠誠履職的精神面貌。我們將會珍而重之，今後亦會繼續堅定地踐行責任和承諾，與其他紀律部隊同心協力，為國家安全、香港穩定和市民福祉作出貢獻。

政府飛行服務隊總監
胡偉雄先生 MBS，GDSM

Controller,
Government Flying Service
Mr West WU Wai-hung, MBS, GDSM

在保安局的領導下，政府飛行服務隊致力為香港市民提供最優質的緊急飛行服務，範圍覆蓋全港、大灣區至南中國海，遠達香港以南 1300 公里。

我們視救急扶危及維護國家安全為使命，堅守「一國兩制」原則，確保香港繁榮穩定，同時亦為大灣區的發展作出貢獻。我對部門的機師、空勤主任、工程師、技術主任及文職同事感到非常自豪，他們敢於面對挑戰，克盡已任，堅守「安全、誠信、服務」的核心價值觀，迎合公眾期望。

期望這本相冊能聯繫您和所有紀律部隊，令您欣賞其專業及無私奉獻，努力不懈地工作，守護香港，使其成為全球最安全的城市。

In the Fire Services Department (FSD), we live by the mission "Serving to save those in distress and protect the community". We strive to perform at our best in firefighting, rescue, ambulance service and fire protection, relentlessly safeguarding the life and property of every citizen. Furthermore, to help address the needs of security and development under the "One Country, Two Systems", and drive Hong Kong's transition from stability to prosperity, the FSD works hard not only to maintain and promote national security, but also to advocate patriotic values, foster youth development, and build a caring and harmonious society.

The candid pictures in this photo album, expertly captured through the lens of the photographer, Dr. Eddy Li, gives the public a genuine and profound portrayal of the FSD in the unwavering pursuit of our mission. We will hold these pictures dear. As we forge ahead, we will continue to fulfil our responsibilities and pledges with determination. Working side by side with other disciplined services, we will play our due part in the quest for national security, Hong Kong's stability and the well-being of our citizens.

Under the leadership of the Security Bureau, the Government Flying Service (GFS) is committed to providing the best professional aviation support and round-the-clock emergency flying service to the people of Hong Kong, covering the Pearl River Delta region and extending beyond Hong Kong to the South China Sea, reaching as far as 1300km south of Hong Kong.

While our core duties revolve around saving lives and responding to emergencies, we stand firm in our commitment to the principle of "One Country, Two Systems" to ensure the stability and prosperity of Hong Kong, seizing the diverse opportunities that emerged from the Greater Bay Area and contribute to its development. I take great pride in my colleagues, the Pilots, Aircrewman Officers, Engineers, Aircraft Technical Officers, and our civilian colleagues who attributed to the success of the GFS. They always go the extra mile to overcome challenges and fulfil their responsibilities, upholding our core values of "Safety, Integrity, and Service", to meet public expectations.

I hope this photo album connects you with all the disciplined services and allows you to appreciate the professionalism and remarkable dedication of our colleagues who work tirelessly to safeguard Hong Kong, making it one of the safest cities globally.

醫療輔助隊總監
林文健醫生 JP

Commissioner of the
Auxiliary Medical Service
Dr Ronald Lam Man-kin, JP

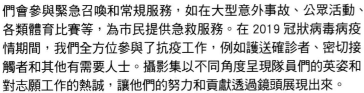

本隊很榮幸能參與李秀恒博士和攝影團隊籌備的攝影集。

醫療輔助隊以成為常規醫療衞生服務的最強後盾、首屈一指的志願應急醫療衞生組織為使命。我們會參與緊急召喚和常規服務，如在大型意外事故、公眾活動、各類體育比賽等，為市民提供急救服務。在 2019 冠狀病毒病疫情期間，我們全方位參與了抗疫工作，例如護送確診者、密切接觸者和其他有需要人士。攝影集以不同角度呈現隊員們的英姿和對志願工作的熱誠，讓他們的努力和貢獻透過鏡頭展現出來。

我藉此機會由衷感謝李博士及攝影團隊，並期望有更多不同人士閱讀這本攝影集，從中領會我們的堅毅與擔當。

民眾安全服務隊處長
羅仁禮先生 MH, JP

Commissioner of the
Civil Aid Service
Mr Lo Yan-lai, MH, JP

民安隊服務香港社會逾七十載，即使時代變遷仍不斷改進，一直堅守「救急扶危，服務社會」的宗旨。民安隊從不停步：在面對災難事故時，我們不分晝夜執行救援工作，為民解困；在平日，我們亦不忘為廣大市民提供各項社區服務。

翻開此相集，細看隊員辛勤工作的每個瞬間，讓我猶如身歷其境，實在別有一番感受。李博士及其攝影團隊拍攝出令人讚嘆的作品，讓市民得以從另一角度窺探保安局轄下各部門的面貌，居功至偉，謹此衷心致謝。

The Auxiliary Medical Service (AMS) is honoured to become part of the Photobook prepared by Dr. LI Sau-hung and his photography team.

Our mission is to provide the strongest support to regular medical and health services and become a premier voluntary, supplementary medical and health services provider. AMS members will participate in emergency situations and regular functions, such as providing first aid services to major incidents, public events and all kinds of sports competitions. During COVID-19, we fully participated in anti-epidemic duties such as escorting confirmed cases, close contacts and other persons in need. The Photobook showcases members' contribution, passion and efforts from different perspectives.

I would like to take this opportunity to express our gratitude to Dr. LI and his photography team again, and hope that more people can appreciate our perseverance and commitment.

Serving Hong Kong for over 70 years, the CAS has been changing and improving its working practices to move with the times. That being said, we always stick to our core mission of providing emergency relief and serving the community. At times of disaster and emergency, we conduct rescue operations round the clock to help those in need; on peaceful days, we work constantly to build resilience and improve citizens' lives at the community level - we never stop.

This photo book took me on a special journey to witness the hard work of CAS members who served the public selflessly. I would like to thank Dr. Li and his team for capturing these stunning images and inviting the public to discover, through their lens, the work of different disciplined services and auxiliary services under the Security Bureau.

慶典

Ceremonies

「同心・展新」紀律部隊暨青少年團體慶國慶七十三周年暨回歸二十五周年步操大匯演

"Together We Prosper" Grand Parade by Disciplined Services and Youth Groups for Celebrating the 73rd Anniversary of the Founding of the People's Republic of China and the 25th Anniversary of the Establishment of the Hong Kong Special Administrative Region

香港特別行政區成立二十六周年升旗儀式上，紀律部隊和飛行服務隊在海上和空中敬禮。

The disciplined services and the Government Flying Service perform a sea parade and a fly-past to mark the 26th Anniversary of the Establishment of the Hong Kong Special Administrative Region at the Flag-Raising Ceremony.

香港特別行政區成立二十六周年升旗儀式上，紀律部隊和飛行服務隊在海上和空中敬禮。

The disciplined services and the Government Flying Service perform a sea parade and a fly-past to mark the 26th Anniversary of the Establishment of the Hong Kong Special Administrative Region at the Flag-Raising Ceremony.

慶祝中華人民共和國香港特別行政區成立二十六周年酒會
Reception to celebrate the 26th Anniversary of the
Establishment of the Hong Kong Special Administrative
Region of the People's Republic of China

憲法四十周年升旗儀式

Flag Raising Ceremony to Commemorate
40th Anniversary of Constitution

慶祝中華人民共和國成立 74 周年紀律部隊及青少年團體匯操暨嘉年華

Parade by Disciplined Services and Youth Groups cum Carnival for
Celebrating the 74th Anniversary of the Founding of the People's
Republic of China

民安隊 70 周年紀念大會操
Celebration of Civil Aid Service (CAS) 70th Anniversary Parade

「同心・展新」紀律部隊暨青少年團體慶國慶七十三周年暨回歸二十五周年步操大
匯演：警察護旗方隊及香港青少年軍

"Together We Prosper" Grand Parade by Disciplined Services and Youth Groups
for Celebrating the 73rd Anniversary of the Founding of the People's Republic of
China and the 25th Anniversary of the Establishment of the Hong Kong Special
Administrative Region: Police Flag Party and Hong Kong Army Cadets

全民國家安全教育日升旗儀式：警察護旗方隊
"National Security Education Day" Flag Raising
Ceremony: Police Flag Party

憲法四十周年升旗儀式：香港海關儀仗隊
Flag Raising Ceremony to Commemorate
40th Anniversary of Constitution: C&ED
Guards of Honour

全民國家安全教育日升旗儀式：警察護旗方隊
"National Security Education Day" Flag
Raising Ceremony: Police Flag Party

「同心・展新」紀律部隊暨青少年團體慶國慶七十三周年暨回歸二十五周年步操大匯演

"Together We Prosper" Grand Parade by Disciplined Services and Youth Groups for Celebrating the 73rd Anniversary of the Founding of the People's Republic of China and the 25th Anniversary of the Establishment of the Hong Kong Special Administrative Region

慶祝中華人民共和國成立 74 周年紀律部隊及青少年團體匯操暨嘉年華

Parade by Disciplined Services and Youth Groups cum Carnival for
Celebrating the 74th Anniversary of the Founding of the People's
Republic of China

「全民國家安全教育日」升旗儀式
Flag Raising Ceremony on
"National Security Education Day"

匯

操

Parades

入境事務學院開放日
Immigration Service Institute of Training
and Development Open Day

「同心‧展新」紀律部隊暨青少年團體慶國慶七十三周年暨回歸二十五周年步操大匯演

"Together We Prosper" Grand Parade by Disciplined Services and Youth Groups for Celebrating the 73rd Anniversary of the Founding of the People's Republic of China and the 25th Anniversary of the Establishment of the Hong Kong Special Administrative Region

「同心・展新」紀律部隊暨青少年團體慶國慶七十三周年暨回歸二十五周年步操大匯演

"Together We Prosper" Grand Parade by Disciplined Services and Youth Groups for Celebrating the 73rd Anniversary of the Founding of the People's Republic of China and the 25th Anniversary of the Establishment of the Hong Kong Special Administrative Region

「同心・展新」紀律部隊暨青少年團體慶國慶七十三周年暨回歸二十五周年步操大匯演

"Together We Prosper" Grand Parade by Disciplined Services and Youth Groups for Celebrating the 73rd Anniversary of the Founding of the People's Republic of China and the 25th Anniversary of the Establishment of the Hong Kong Special Administrative Region

香港海關儀仗隊

C&ED Guards of Honour

消防處儀仗隊（紅色飾帶）、懲教署儀仗隊（黃色飾帶）
及警察儀仗隊（白色飾帶）

The Fire Services Department's Guard of Honour (Red Lanyard), Correctional Services Department's Guard of Honour (Yellow Lanyard) and Police Guard of Honour (White Lanyard)

懲教署儀仗隊（黃色飾帶）及警察儀仗隊（白色飾帶）

The Correctional Services Department's Guard of Honour (Yellow Lanyard) and Police Guard of Honour (White Lanyard)

慶祝中華人民共和國成立 74 周年紀律部隊及青少年
團體匯操暨嘉年華

Parade by Disciplined Services and Youth Groups
cum Carnival for Celebrating the 74th Anniversary
of the Founding of the People's Republic of China

消防處儀仗隊
Fire Services Department's
Guard of Honour

警察儀仗隊
Police Guard of Honour

警察儀仗隊
Police Guard of Honour

入境事務處儀仗隊
Immigration Department's Guard of Honour

香港海關儀仗隊
C&ED Guards of Honour

懲教署儀仗隊
The Correctional Services Department's Guard of Honour

消防處儀仗隊
Fire Services Department's
Guard of Honour

香港海關儀仗隊
C&ED Guards of Honour

入境事務處儀仗隊
Immigration Department's Guard of Honour

入境事務處青少年領袖團
Immigration Department Youth Leaders Corps

少年警訊
JPC

海關青年領袖團
Customs Youth Leader Corps

醫療輔助隊少年團
Auxiliary Medical Service (AMS) Cadet Corps

懲教署更生先鋒領袖
The Correctional Services Department's
"Rehabilitation Pioneer Leaders"

消防及救護青年團
Fire and Ambulance Services Teen Connect

民安隊少年團儀仗隊
Cadet Corps Guard of Honour

香港航空青年團
Hong Kong Air Cadet Corps

香港青少年軍總會
Hong Kong Army Cadets Association

「全民國家安全教育日」警察學院開放日
Hong Kong Police College Open Day on
"National Security Education Day"

「全民國家安全教育日」警察學院開放日
Hong Kong Police College Open Day on
"National Security Education Day"

入境事務學院開放日
Immigration Service Institute of Training
and Development Open Day

入境事務學院開放日
Immigration Service Institute of Training
and Development Open Day

懲教署「家・國・懲」大匯演暨開放日

Correctional Services Department holds Grand
Performance cum Open Day

「全民國家安全教育日」警察學院開放日

Hong Kong Police College Open Day on
"National Security Education Day"

「全民國家安全教育日」警察學院開放日
Hong Kong Police College Open Day on
"National Security Education Day"

消防處儀仗隊參與結業會操

The Fire Services Department's Guard of Honour
takes part in passing-out parade.

慶祝中華人民共和國成立 74 周年紀律部隊及青少年團
體匯操暨嘉年華

Parade by Disciplined Services and Youth Groups cum
Carnival for Celebrating the 74th Anniversary of the
Founding of the People's Republic of China

入境事務學院開放日
Immigration Service Institute of Training and
Development Open Day

民安隊新隊員結業會操
CAS Recruits Passing-out Parade

爆炸品處理課
Explosive Ordnance Disposal Bureau

政府飛行服務隊機隊：龐巴迪挑戰者 605

Government Flying Service Aircraft:
Bombardier Challenger 605

政府飛行服務隊機隊：空中巴士 H175
Government Flying Service Aircraft: Airbus H175

警務處船隊：中型巡邏警輪
Police Fleet: Medium Patrol Launch

警務處船隊：分區快速巡邏小艇
Police Fleet: Divisional Fast Patrol Craft

警務處船隊：總區訓練警輪
Police Fleet: Regional Training Launch

海關船隊：區域巡邏船及高速截擊艇

Customs Fleet: Sector Patrol Launch
and High Speed Pursuit Craft

海關船隊：高速截擊艇
Customs Fleet: High Speed Pursuit Craft

海關船隊：高速截擊艇
Customs Fleet: High Speed Pursuit Craft

海關船隊：海騎式橡皮艇
Customs Fleet: Sea-rider Inflatable Craft

海關船隊：高速截擊艇
Customs Fleet: High Speed Pursuit Craft

消防船：十一號滅火輪
Fire boat: Fireboat 11

懲教署「善衛號」
Correctional Services Department "Seaward"

入境船：「入境一號」
Immigration Launch: "IMM 1"

消防船：潛水支援快艇（二號）（前）、十一號滅火輪（中）
及七號滅火輪（後）

Fire Boat: Diving Support Speedboat (Diving 2)(Left),
Fireboat 11 (Middle) and Fireboat 7 (Right)

消防船：十一號滅火輪（左）、七號滅火輪（中）及
潛水支援快艇（二號）（右）

Fire boat: Fireboat 11 (Left), Fireboat 7 (Middle) and
Diving Support Speedboat (Diving 2) (Right)

消防船：潛水支援快艇（二號）（左）、七號滅火輪（中）及十一號滅火輪（右）

Fire boat: Diving Support Speedboat (Diving2) (Left), Fireboat 7 (Middle) and Fireboat 11 (Right)

消防及救護設備：後勤支援車
Fire and Ambulance Appliances:
Logistic Support Appliance

香港消防處　Fire Services Depa

消防及救護設備：滅火機械人
Fire and Ambulance Appliances:
Firefighting Robot

消防及救護設備：迷你搶救車
Fire and Ambulance Appliances:
Mini Rescue Truck

消防及救護設備：流動指揮車及無人機
Fire and Ambulance Appliances: Mobile
Command Unit and Drone

消防
FIRE

A 級化學物品保護袍（A 袍）
Level A Chemical Protection Suit (CPS)

B 級化學物品保護袍（B 袍）
Level B Chemical Protection Suit (CPS)

慶祝中華人民共和國成立 74 周年紀律部隊及青少年團體匯操暨嘉年華
Parade by Disciplined Services and Youth Groups cum Carnival for Celebrating the 74th Anniversary of the Founding of the People's Republic of China

旅行證件印製中心
Travel Document Personalisation Centre

自助出入境檢查（e-道）服務
Automated Immigration Clearance
(e-Channel) Service

非觸式 e- 道
Contactless e-Channel

港珠澳大橋管制站
Hong Kong-Zhuhai-Macao Bridge Control Point

車廂及車窗
開車窗及
車廂燈

Please open the
windows and
switch on the
interior lights

香港海關入境車輛 X 光檢查大樓
C&ED Inbound Vehicle
X-ray Inspection Building

香港海關入境車輛 X 光檢查大樓

C&ED Inbound Vehicle X-ray
Inspection Building

香港海關智慧化系統和儀器
C&ED smart systems and equipment

懲教署以科技協助監管在囚人士。

The Correctional Services Department utilises technologies to assist in the supervision of persons in custody.

香港懲教學院電子課室
The "e-classroom" in the Hong Kong Correctional Services Academy

香港懲教學院「心戰室」
The "e-theatre" in the Hong Kong Correctional Services Academy

爆炸品處理課
Explosive Ordnance Disposal Bureau

入境處船隻搜查小組
IMMD Ship Searching Unit

138

「迅捷 2021」跨部門大型交通意外事故聯合演習
"QUICKSKILL 2021" major traffic incident exercise

「棋盤三」大亞灣應變計劃
"Checkerboard III" Daya Bay Contingency Plan Exercise

「迅捷 2021」跨部門大型交通意外事故聯合演習
"QUICKSKILL 2021" major traffic incident exercise

「迅捷 2021」跨部門大型交通意外事故聯合演習
"QUICKSKILL 2021" major traffic incident exercise

消防處災難應變救援隊演習
FSD Disaster Response and Rescue Team (DRRT)

消防處災難應變救援隊演習
FSD Disaster Response and Rescue Team (DRRT)

往北角/寶琳 ② →
to North Point/Po Lam

綠色類別
傷者接收站
Green Case
Casualty
Collecting Point

港鐵事故消防及救護演習
MTR incident fire and ambulance drills

消防處飛機事故及救援演習
FSD Aircraft Crash and Rescue Exercise

飛機事故及救援演習
Aircraft Crash and Rescue Exercise

消防處災難應變救援隊演習
FSD Disaster Response and Rescue Team (DRRT)

消防救援演習
Fire and rescue exercise

跨部門山火暨攀山拯救行動演習
Inter-departmental vegetation fire
and mountain rescue exercise

跨部門山火暨攀山拯救行動演習
Inter-departmental vegetation fire
and mountain rescue exercise

跨部門山火暨攀山拯救行動演習
Inter-departmental vegetation fire
and mountain rescue exercise

「迅捷 2021」跨部門大型交通意外事故聯合演習
"QUICKSKILL 2021" major traffic incident exercise

夜間海上搜救演習
Maritime search and rescue exercise at night

夜間海上搜救演習
Maritime search and rescue exercise at night

衝鋒隊戰術演練
Emergency Unit tactics training exercise

紀律部隊工作犬展示

Demonstrations by the disciplined services' working dogs

懲教署工作犬展示
Demonstration by the working dog of the
Correctional Services Department

胡椒噴劑展示
Demonstration of using pepper spray

懲教署工作犬展示

Demonstration by the working dog of the
Correctional Services Department

清理塌樹展示
Demonstration of collapsed tree clearance

海關手持式車輛掃描機展示
C&ED Demonstration of portable vehicle scanner

安
保

Security

反恐特勤隊巡邏
Counter Terrorism Response Unit patrol

反恐演習
Counter-terrorism exercise

反恐演習
Counter-terrorism exercise

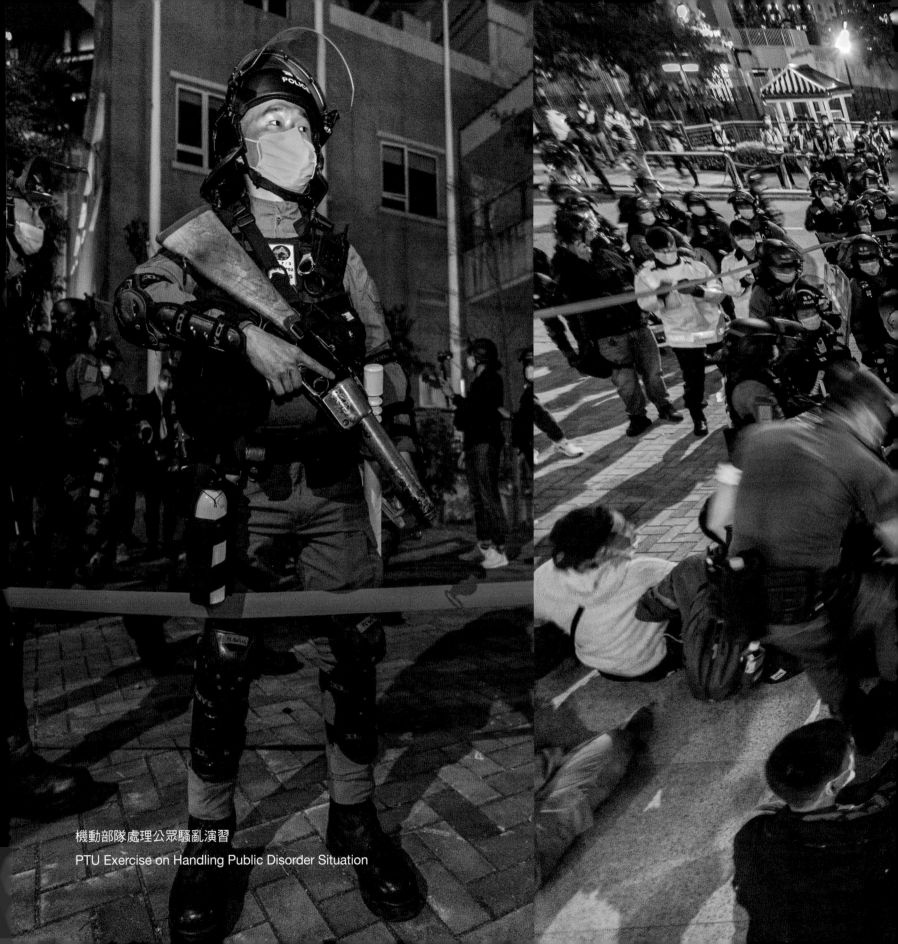

機動部隊處理公眾騷亂演習

PTU Exercise on Handling Public Disorder Situation

機動部隊處理公眾騷亂演習
PTU Exercise on Handling Public Disorder Situation

機動部隊處理公眾騷亂演習
PTU Exercise on Handling Public Disorder Situation

機動部隊處理公眾騷亂演習
PTU Exercise on Handling Public Disorder Situation

機動部隊處理公眾騷亂演習
PTU Exercise on Handling Public Disorder Situation

懲教署區域應變隊進行防暴演習。
An anti-riot drill conducted by the Regional Response Team of the Correctional Services Department.

訓
練

Training

警察槍械訓練

Police weapons training

海關槍械訓練
C&ED weapons training

懲教署槍械訓練
Weapons training of the Correctional
Services Department

特別任務連槍械訓練
SDU weapons training

海關槍械訓練
C&ED weapons training

警察槍械訓練
Police weapons training

懲教署槍械訓練
Weapons training of the Correctional
Services Department

懲教署槍械訓練
Weapons training of the Correctional
Services Department

特別任務連訓練
SDU training

特別任務連訓練
SDU training

特別任務連訓練
SDU training

特別任務連訓練
SDU training

特別任務連訓練
SDU training

入境處緊急應變隊訓練

IMMD emergency response team training

入境處緊急應變隊訓練
IMMD emergency response team training

入境處緊急應變隊訓練
IMMD emergency response team training

海關搜查犬訓練
Training of Customs detector dogs

懲教署工作犬訓練
Working dog's training of the Correctional
Services Department

消防訓練
Fire services training

消防訓練
Fire services training

特別任務連與飛行服務隊聯合訓練
SDU and GFS joint training

海關潛水隊訓練

Customs Diving Team training

懲教署入職訓練
CSD recruit training

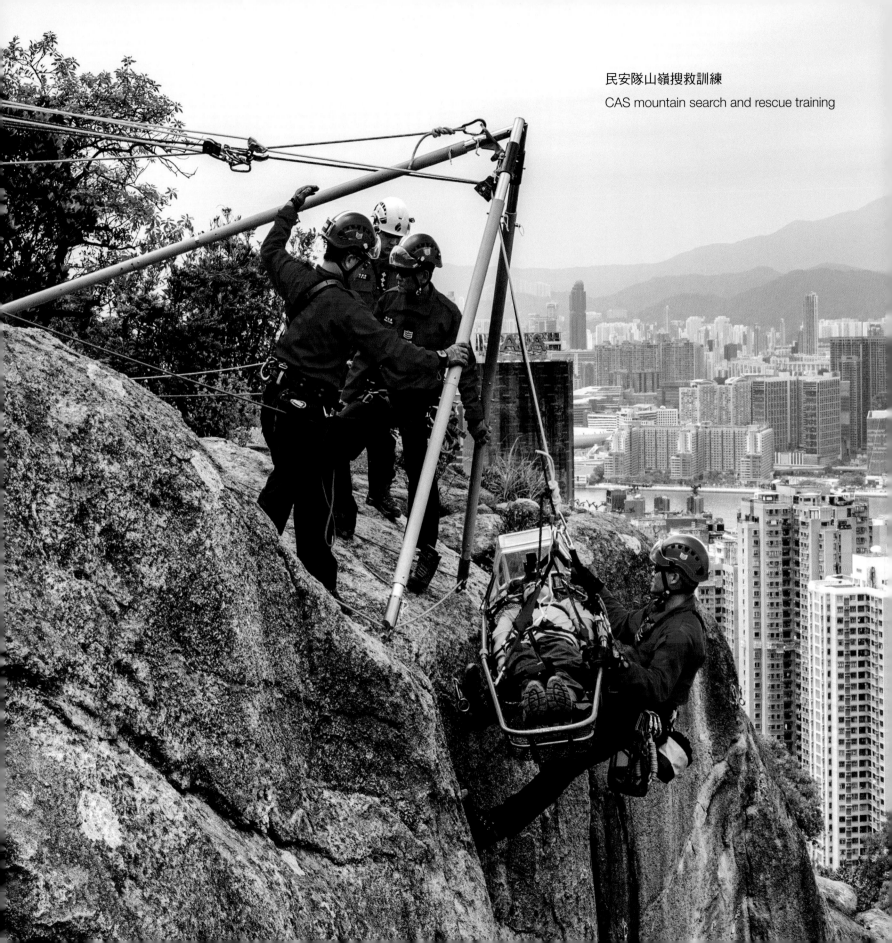

民安隊山嶺搜救訓練
CAS mountain search and rescue training

民安隊緊急救援訓練
CAS emergency rescue training

守護

Protection

蘭桂坊除夕倒數人群管理

Crowd management measures on New
Year's Eve Countdown at Lan Kwai Fong

香港特別行政區救援隊赴土耳其救災返港儀式

Welcome Ceremony for The Hong Kong
Special Administrative Region Search and
Rescue Team Returning from Türkiye

反罪惡行動
Anti-crime operations

反罪惡行動
Anti-crime operations

反罪惡行動
Anti-crime operations

反罪惡行動
Anti-crime operations

反罪惡行動
Anti-crime operations

衝鋒隊巡邏
Emergency Unit patrol

衝鋒隊巡邏
Emergency Unit patrol

「香港國際七人欖球賽」搜查行動

Search operation for the "Hong Kong Sevens"

「香港國際七人欖球賽」搜查行動
Search operation for the "Hong Kong Sevens"

「香港國際七人欖球賽」搜查行動
Search operation for the "Hong Kong Sevens"

指紋檢驗
Fingerprint examination

撲滅火警
Firefighting

入境處船隻搜查小組行動
IMMD Ship Searching Unit operation

入境處船隻搜查小組行動
IMMD Ship Searching Unit operation

入境處船隻搜查小組行動
IMMD Ship Searching Unit operation

入境處船隻搜查小組行動
IMMD Ship Searching Unit operation

入境處船隻搜查小組行動
IMMD Ship Searching Unit operation

出入境檢查
Immigration clearance

出入境檢查
Immigration clearance

海關入境私家車檢查
C&ED inbound private car examination

海關入境貨物檢查
C&ED inbound cargo examination

海關及食環署聯合行動
C&ED and FEHD joint operation

海關打擊盜版執法行動
C&ED anti-piracy enforcement

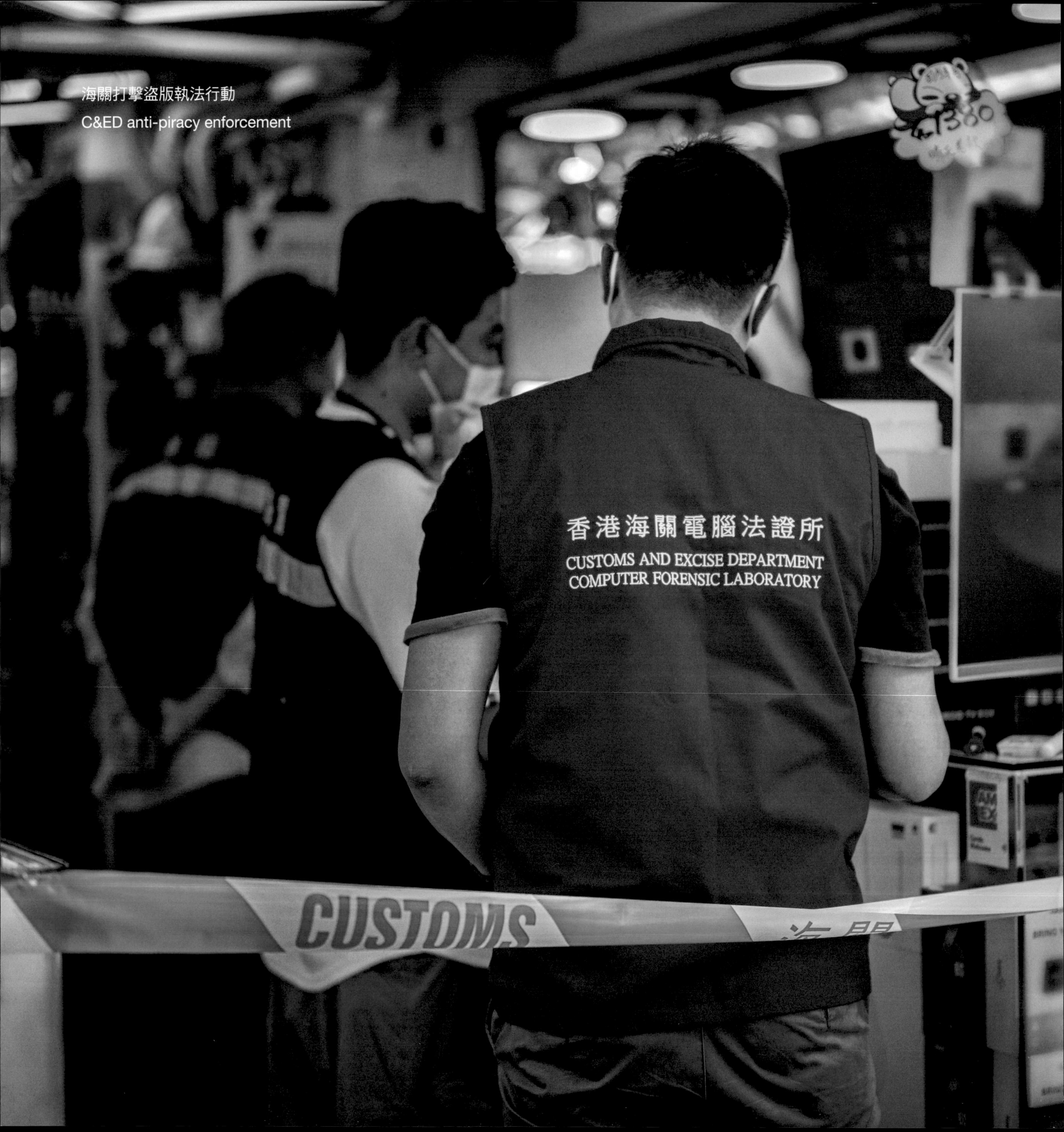

海關打擊盜版執法行動

C&ED anti-piracy enforcement

海關艘船及貨物小組
Customs Ship Search and Cargo Unit

海關艘船及貨物小組
Customs Ship Search and Cargo Unit

醫療輔助隊為「2023 渣打香港馬拉松」提供急救醫療服務

Auxiliary Medical Service (AMS) provides first-aid medical services
to assist the Standard Chartered Hong Kong Marathon 2023

醫療輔助隊為 2022「新鴻基地產香港單車節」提供急
救醫療服務

Auxiliary Medical Service (AMS) provides first-aid
medical services to assist the 2022 Sun Hung Kai
Properties Hong Kong Cyclothon

急救示範

Demonstration of first-aid provision

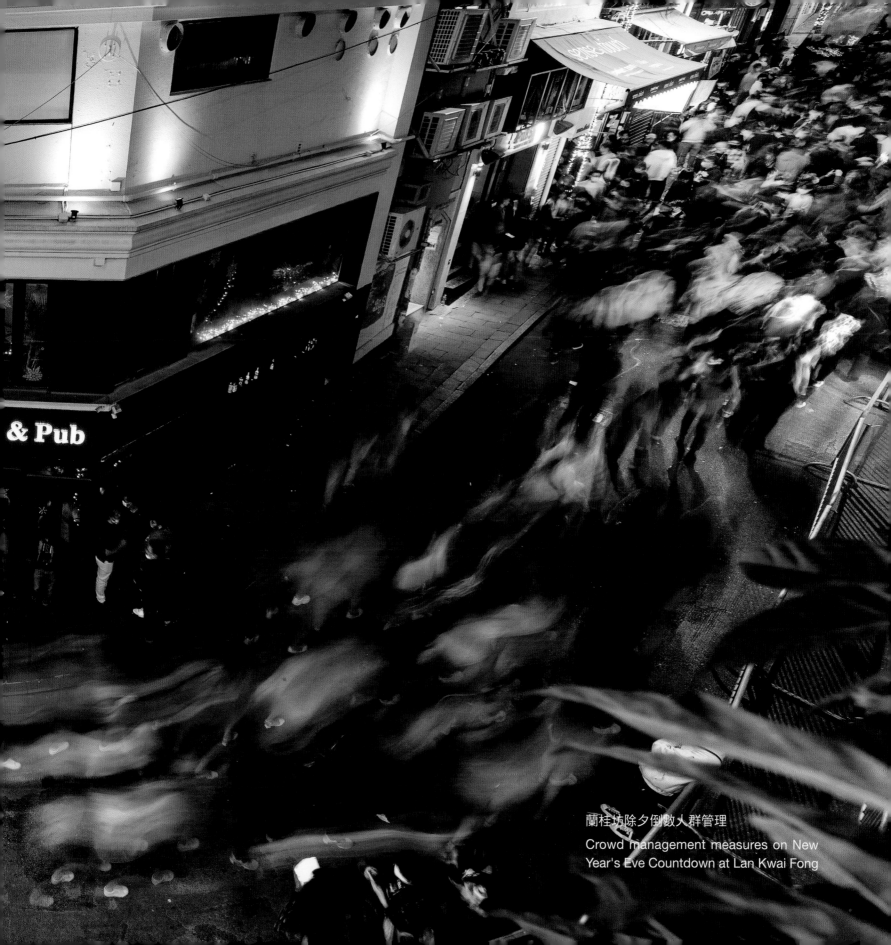

& Pub

蘭桂坊除夕倒數人群管理
Crowd management measures on New
Year's Eve Countdown at Lan Kwai Fong

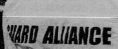

「香港國際七人欖球賽」人群管理
Crowd management measures
at the "Hong Kong Sevens"

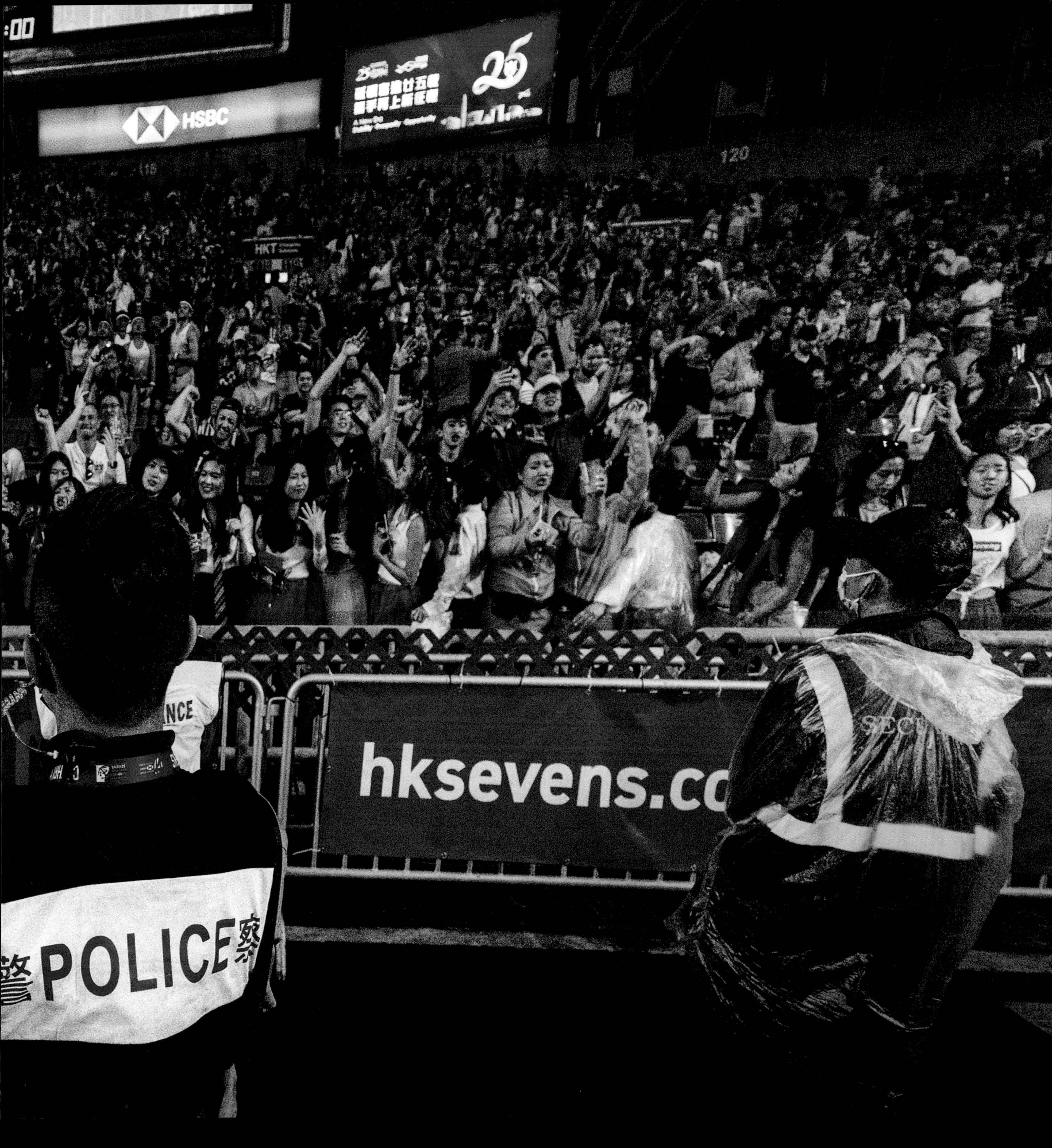
HSBC
25
120
HKT
hksevens.co
警POLICE察

「香港國際七人欖球賽」人群管理
Crowd management measures at
the "Hong Kong Sevens"

「香港國際七人欖球賽」人群管理
Crowd management measures at
the "Hong Kong Sevens"

「香港國際龍舟邀請賽」人群管理
Crowd Managetment measures at the "Hong Kong International Dragon Boat Races"

沙頭角分區巡邏
Sha Tau Kok Division patrol

大澳端午龍舟遊涌人群管理
Crowd management measures at Tai O Dragon Boat Water Parade

長洲太平清醮人群管理
Crowd management measures at Cheung Chau Jiao Festival

年宵市場人群管理行動
Crowd management measures at
Chinese New Year Flower Market

農曆新年黃大仙祠人群管理行動
Crowd management measures
at Wong Tai Sin Temple during
Chinese New Year

年宵市場人群管理行動
Crowd management measures at
Chinese New Year Flower Market

旅客清關檢查
Passenger clearance

毌 ⋯⋯ 通道
沒有 ⋯⋯ / 受管制物品

Nothing to declare
Without dutiable / controlled items to declare

↑ 出口 Exit

出口 EXIT Auto door

旅客清關檢查
Passenger clearance

海關機場突擊搜查隊
C&ED Airport Strike and Search Unit

懲教人員致力守護香港刑事司法體系的最後防線。

Correctional officers are committed to guarding the last element of Hong Kong's criminal justice system.

赤柱
Stanle

赤柱東
99 Tung

教　育

Education

香港懲教博物館副館——社區教育體驗館
The Annex to the Hong Kong Correctional Services
Museum - Community Education Experience Centre

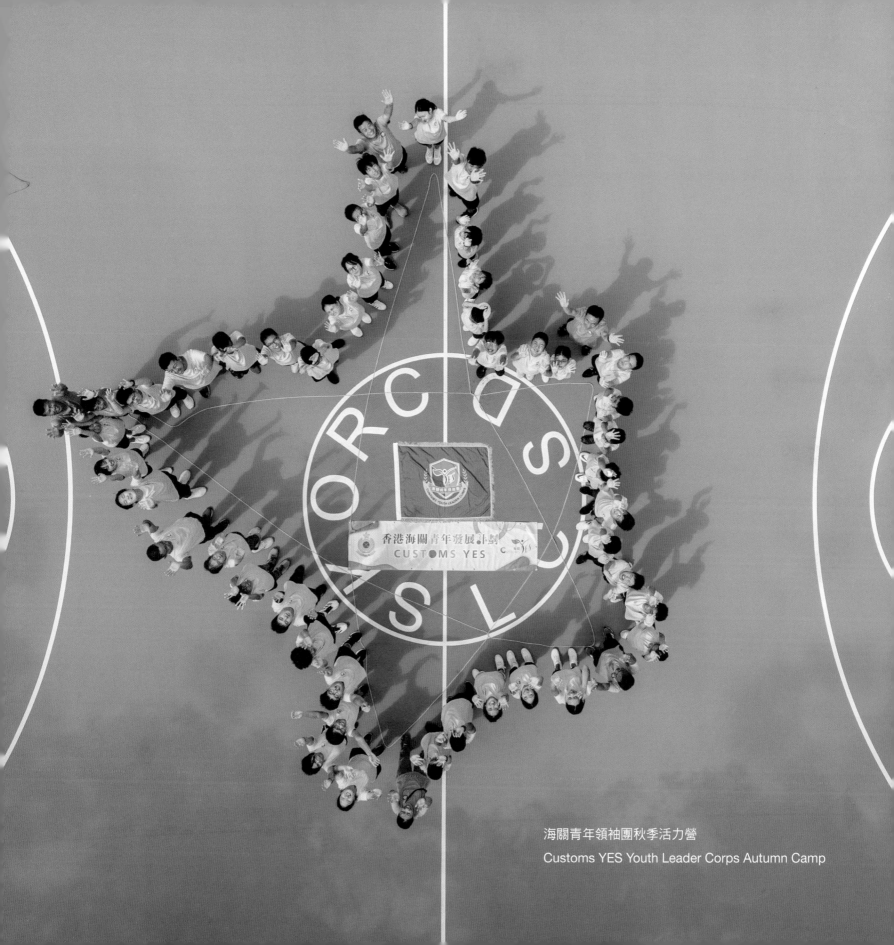

海關青年領袖團秋季活力營
Customs YES Youth Leader Corps Autumn Camp

懲教署通過「更生先鋒計劃」下的社區教育活動培養學生的正確價值觀。

The community education activities under the Correctional Services Department's "Rehabilitation Pioneer Project" help foster positive values among students.

愛護家國、奉公守法、遠離毒品、支持更生」
Safeguarding Our Country and Home
Leading a Law-abiding and Drug- free Life
Supporting offender Rehabilitation
The Correctional Services Dep

懲教署通過「更生先鋒計劃」下的社區教育活動培養學生的正確價值觀。

The community education activities under the Correctional Services Department's "Rehabilitation Pioneer Project" help foster positive values among students.

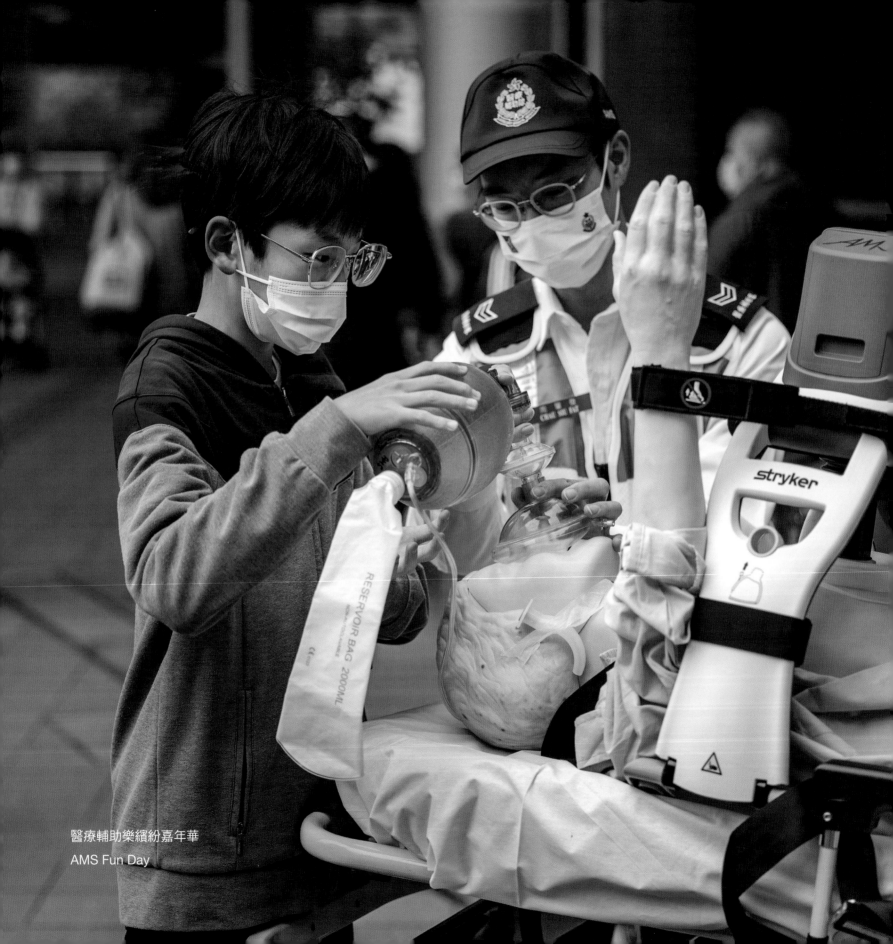

醫療輔助樂繽紛嘉年華
AMS Fun Day

醫療輔助樂繽紛嘉年華
AMS Fun Day

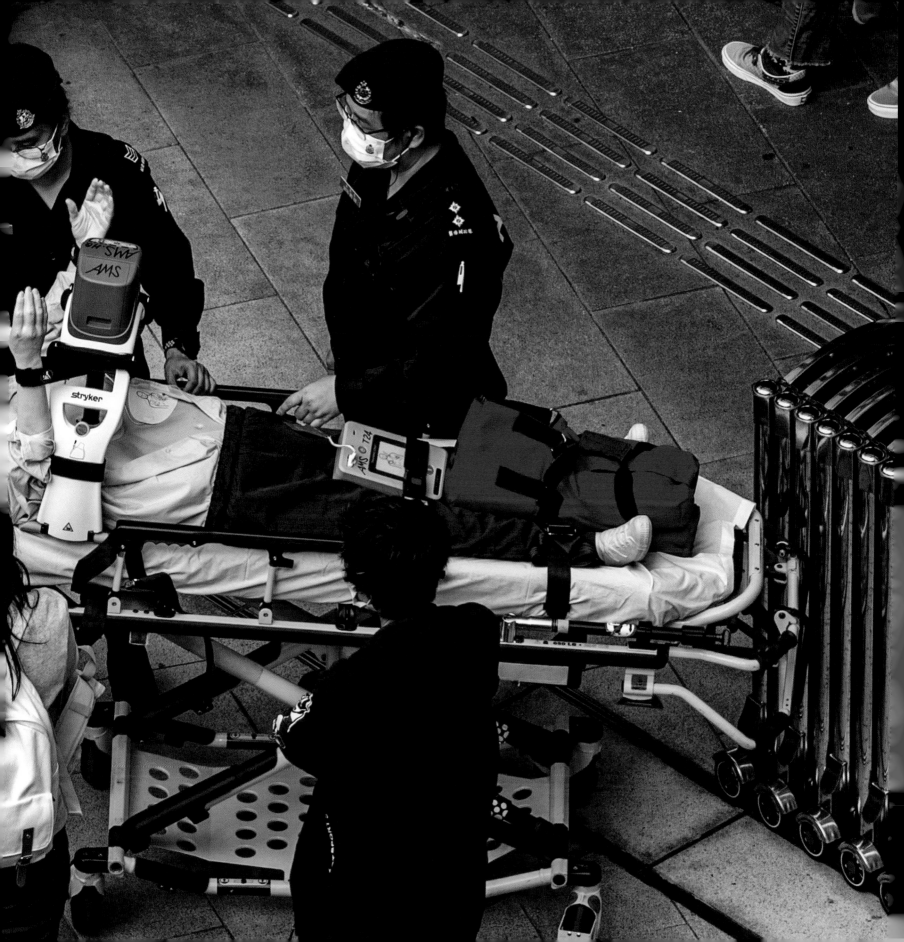

心肺復甦法
去顫器
體驗區

慶祝中華人民共和國成立 74 周年紀律部
隊及青少年團體匯操暨嘉年華 - 醫療輔
助隊攤位遊戲

Parade by Disciplined Services
and Youth Groups cum Carnival for
Celebrating the 74th Anniversary of the
Founding of the People's Republic of
China - AMS's Game Booth

民安隊少年團領袖培訓
CAS Cadet Corps Leadership Training

民安隊少年團獨木舟訓練

CAS Cadet Corps Kayak Training

懲教署「家‧國‧懲」大匯演暨開放日
Correctional Services Department holds Grand
Performance cum Open Day

入境事務處青少年領袖團參觀旅行證件印製中心
Immigration Department Youth Leaders Corps visits
the Travel Document Personalisation Centre

「全民國家安全教育日」警察學院開放日
Hong Kong Police College Open Day on
"National Security Education Day"

更生
Rehabilitation

懲教署為在囚人士舉辦親子活動。
The Correctional Services Department organises parent-child activities for persons in custody.

懲教署為年長在囚人士推行綜合懲教計劃，協助
他們獲釋後重新融入社會。

The Correctional Services Department
implements an integrated correctional
programme to help elderly persons in custody
reintegrate into society after release.

在囚人士醫療護理
Medical treatment for persons in custody

懲教署為在囚人士提供多元化的職業訓練課程。

The Correctional Services Department
provides diversified vocational training
courses for persons in custody.

在囚人士教育
Education for persons in custody

在囚人士通過參與廚房工作培養良好習慣。
Persons in custody develop good habits through engaging in kitchen work.

沙咀懲教所
SHA TSUI CORRECTIONAL INSTITUTION

年輕在囚人士學習舞獅。
Young persons in custody are
learning lion dance.

年輕在囚人士練習中式步操。

Young persons in custody are practising the Chinese-style foot drill.

懲教署的監管服務

Supervision services provided by the
Correctional Services Department

關愛
Caring

香港特別行政區救援隊赴土耳其救災返港儀式
Welcome Ceremony for The Hong Kong
Special Administrative Region Search and
Rescue Team Returning from Türkiye

民安隊竹篙灣社區隔離設施
CAS Penny's Bay Community Isolation Facility

民安隊竹篙灣社區隔離設施
CAS Penny's Bay Community Isolation Facility

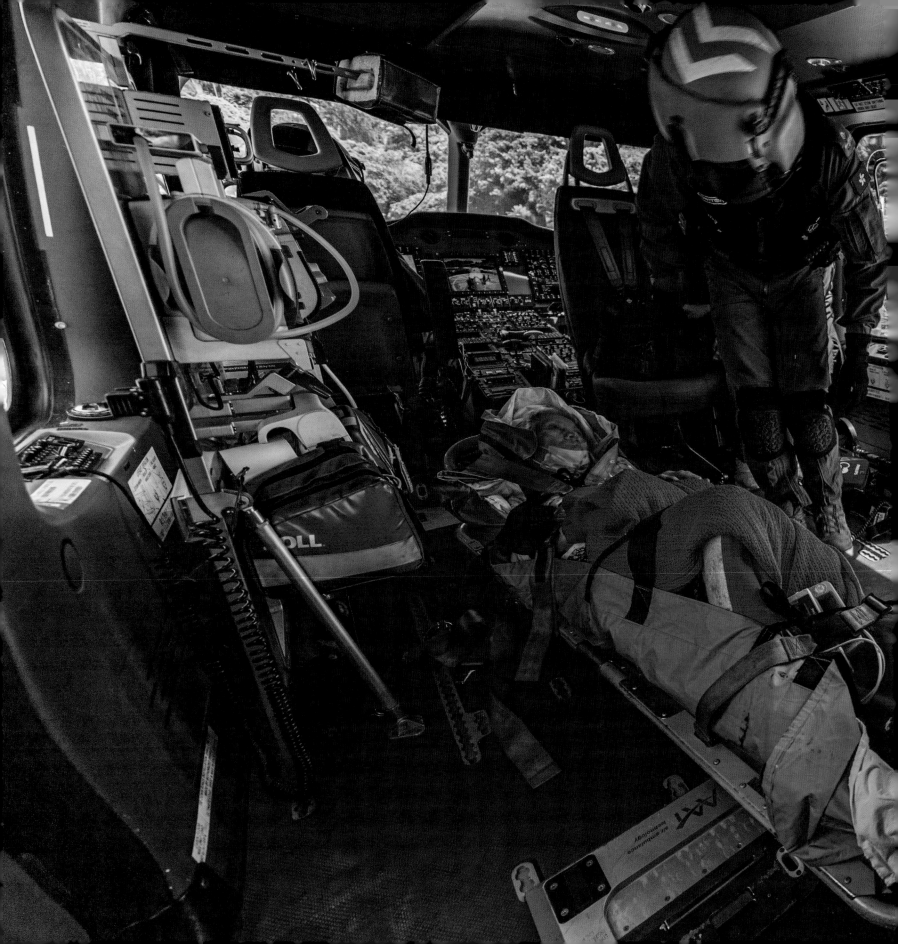

飛行服務隊空中救護
GFS Air Ambulance

農曆新年期間醫療輔助隊及民安隊駐車公廟提供支援

AMS & CAS provide on-site support at the Che Kung Temple during the Chinese New Year

大澳端午龍舟遊涌人群管理

Crowd management measures at Tai O
Dragon Boat Water Parade

醫療輔助隊在新冠疫情期間於安老院舍撤離行動
AMS Evacuation Operation at elderly home during Covid-19 period

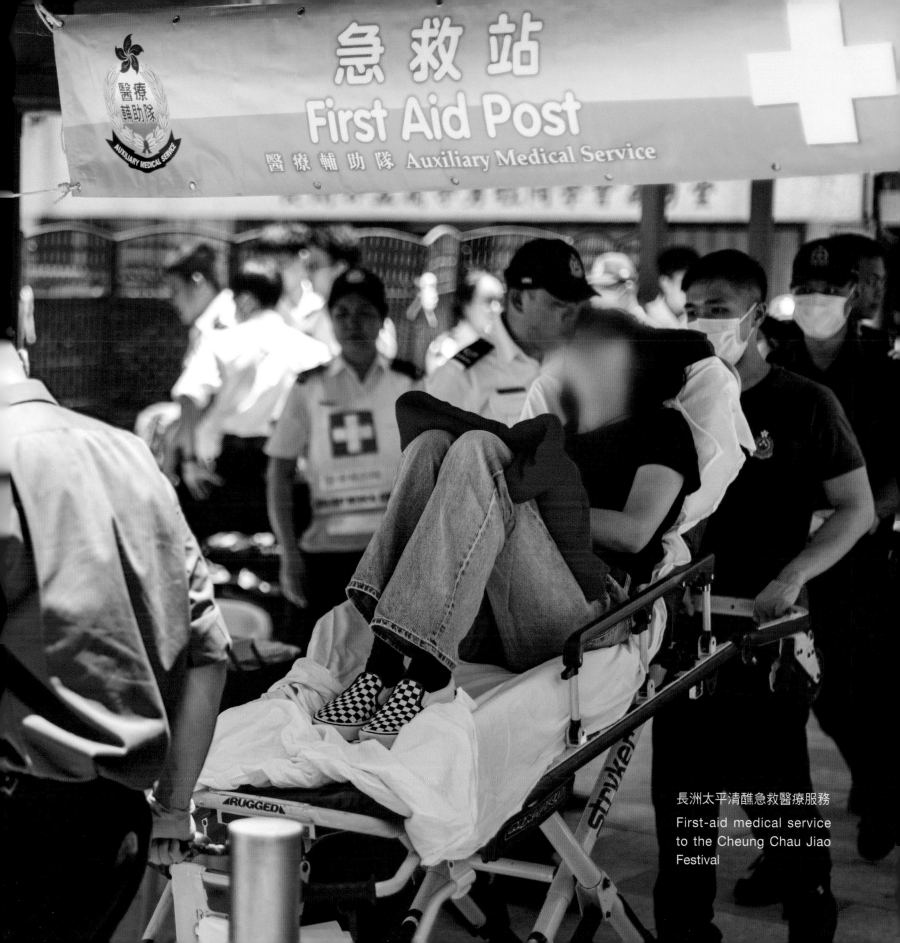

急救站
First Aid Post
醫療輔助隊 Auxiliary Medical Service

長洲太平清醮急救醫療服務
First-aid medical service to the Cheung Chau Jiao Festival

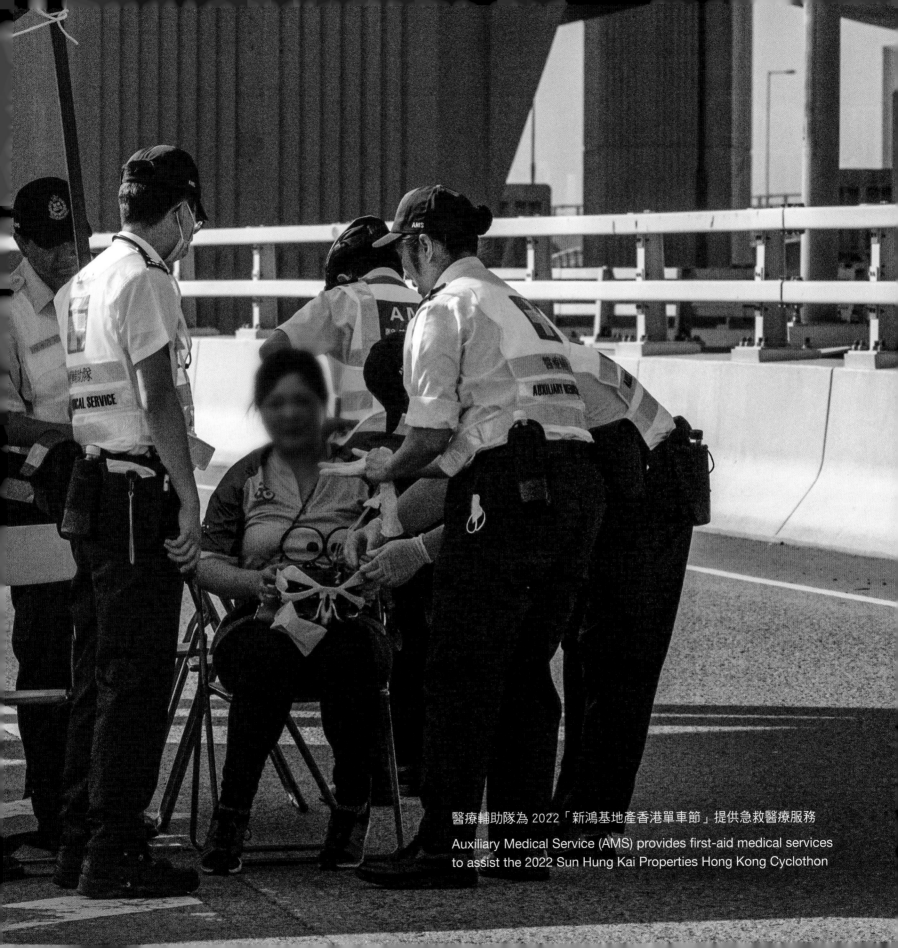

醫療輔助隊為 2022「新鴻基地產香港單車節」提供急救醫療服務

Auxiliary Medical Service (AMS) provides first-aid medical services
to assist the 2022 Sun Hung Kai Properties Hong Kong Cyclothon

反恐特勤隊巡邏

Counter Terrorism Response Unit Patrol

慶祝中華人民共和國成立 74 周年紀律部
隊及青少年團體匯操暨嘉年華攤位遊戲

Parade by Disciplined Services
and Youth Groups cum Carnival for
Celebrating the 74th Anniversary of the
Founding of the People's Republic of
China Game Booths

懲教署「家・國・懲」大匯演暨開放日
Correctional Services Department holds
Grand Performance cum Open Day

慶祝中華人民共和國成立 74 周年紀律部隊及青少年團體匯操暨嘉年華攤位遊戲

Parade by Disciplined Services and Youth Groups cum Carnival for Celebrating the 74th Anniversary of the Founding of the People's Republic of China Game Booths

出入境檢查
Immigration clearance

警察學院結業會操
Police passing-out parade

懲教署「家·國·懲」大匯演暨開放日
Correctional Services Department holds
Grand Performance cum Open Day

2023 沙頭角龍舟邀請賽
Sha Tau Kok Dragon Boat
Races 2023

長洲太平清醮
Cheung Chau Jiao
Festival

作者的話
Author's Message

李秀恒
Eddy Li

二零二三年·秋
Autumn, 2023

中國香港
Hong Kong, China

在一個研討會上，有位年輕朋友問我人生追求的目標，我思索片刻後回答：「光陰有限，但生活的樂趣是無限，如何利用有限的時間，做無限有趣、有意義的事情，才不枉此生。」

常言道「冇錢」不行，在面對生活開支和照顧家庭時，努力工作賺錢是非常重要的。然而，無止境地追求財富，成為金錢的奴隸，並不能賦予人生真正的意義。「修身齊家」是一個正常的目標，但在工作和生活之外，投入時間和力量服務社會，為大眾做出貢獻，為我們深愛的城市香港發光發熱，更可為人生歷程寫下刻骨銘心的紀錄。

經歷了社會事件和疫情的考驗，我們進一步認識到人身安全和健康的可貴。幸運的是，我們身邊有一群紀律部隊和輔助部隊的朋友堅守最前線，勇於面對危險和惡劣的工作環境，辛勤工作，守護這座七百多萬人城市的安寧。

作為一個曾為「國家地理」出版攝影集的攝影師，我拿起了手中的相機，表達內心的感受，讓大眾了解香港紀律部隊及輔助部隊有素的訓練、先進的裝備，更重要的是他們以服務市民為本的初衷，心繫不移地達成他們的「使命」。慶幸能夠近距離觀察及紀錄香港保安局同事們的工作，並透過我的鏡頭，在不同角度下把它們展示出來。

從數萬張心血照片中，挑選了近三百張作品出版，整整一年半的拍攝過程，深入認識及體會到他們辛勤、專業工作背後的熱誠、擔當以及守護我們家園的責任感。我和我的團隊付出了大量的時間和汗水，但我們很高興能藉著這輯相集，向所有香港紀律部隊及輔助部隊人員致敬，使讀者能夠通過相集裏的影像及故事，自豪地與他們並肩，感恩生活在這個進步的城市，一起說好「香港故事」。

I was once asked at a seminar by a young audience about the goals of my life's pursuits. After a short pondering, my reply was, "Time is limited, but the joys of life are infinite. To use the limited time to engage in unlimited interesting and meaningful endeavors is how you make your life a worthwhile trip."

It is often said that "money is essential." When faced with expenses of living and taking care of families, working hard for money is by no means piddling. However, the endless pursuit of wealth can only turn one into a slave to money, imposing barely any meaning to our lives. As the old Chinese saying goes, "Cultivate the self, regulate the family" are simply the essential goal, but beyond work and life, sparing time and efforts to serve the society, contributing to the public and offering what I have to our beloved city of Hong Kong, enable us to carve an unforgettable engravement to our journey of life.

Having stood the test of violent riots and the pandemic, we have come to further appreciate the value of personal safety and health. Fortunately enough, we have, by our sides, a group of disciplined and auxiliary services guarding at the forefront, despite of extreme danger and adverse working environment. Their diligence has safeguarded the peacefulness of this city with over seven million people.

As a photographer who has previously published photography collections for the "National Geographic", I try to express my inner feelings through my cameras, showing the public the well-trained disciplinary and auxiliary services in Hong Kong, as well as their professional equipment, and, most importantly, their unwavering commitment to serving the citizens and their tireless effort to fulfill their "mission." It was lucky for me to have the opportunity to closely observe and document the work of Hong Kong Security Bureau, and present them through my lens from different perspectives.

From the original tens of thousands of photos, I have selected nearly three hundred for publication. A year and a half's photo-taking process has enabled me to understand and experience the dedication, responsibility sense of duty behind their hard work and professionalism in protecting our homeland. My team and I have put in a great amount of time and effort, yet we are delighted to pay tribute to all the members of the Hong Kong disciplinary and auxiliary services through this photography collection. We hope that readers can proudly stand shoulder to shoulder with them, expressing gratitude for living in this progressive city and together, tell a great "Hong Kong story."

鳴謝 Acknowledgements

Peter Penn, Gilbert Yu, Christina Tam, Derek Lee, Chan Chi Fai, Charles Lam, Regis Cheng, Johnny Lee, Benny Wong, Albert Young, Ken Li